Mrs. Pepperpot's Outing

Other books by Alf Prøysen include:

MRS. PEPPERPOT IN THE MAGIC WOOD

MRS. PEPPERPOT TO THE RESCUE

Mrs. Pepperpot's Outing

by Alf Prøysen

Retold by Marianne Helweg

Illustrated by Björn Berg

PANTHEON BOOKS

Chapter One

IT WAS A BEAUTIFUL sunny summer morning, and
Mrs. Pepperpot was standing at her kitchen window
peeling onions. You remember Mrs. Pepperpot? She's
the little old woman who lives on a hillside in Norway
and has the habit of shrinking to the size of a pepperpot at the most inconvenient moments.

Well, here she was, peeling onions, and from time
to time she sniffed a little, the way people do when
they are peeling onions. As the tears rolled down her
cheeks she wiped them away with the back of her
hand and sighed. She was not feeling very happy.

But Mr. Pepperpot was; he was on vacation. Now
he came rushing through the door with his hat askew,
and his hair all over the place. Waving his arms, he
shouted: "I've got news for you, Mrs. P.! Guess what
it is?"

"Good news?" said Mrs. Pepperpot. "Have you
found me a new pet?" Because she had just been

thinking how empty and sad the house was without even a cat or a dog.

"No, no, something *much* better. You'll have to have another guess," said her husband. "Pets! How can you be so old-fashioned? They're a dead loss when you want to go away anywhere, always needing to be fed and looked after."

"But I *like* looking after animals, they're fun," she answered. "Besides, quite often one doesn't really *want* to go away, and then it's very useful to be able to say you have to look after the animals." She wiped away another tear. "Oh, those onions!"

"Well, I think you're behind the times," said Mr. Pepperpot. "It's good for everyone to get about and not be stuck in one place all your life."

This made Mrs. Pepperpot laugh. "Did you say get about? How far do we get in your old wreck of a car? The person who's stuck in one place is *you*, with your head under the car's hood every night for weeks on end!"

"It's my hobby," said Mr. Pepperpot, "everyone should have a hobby nowadays. It says in the paper you should make good use of your free time."

You see, Mr. Pepperpot had bought an old car

cheaply, and ever since he had been tinkering with it, putting in new parts and cleaning and polishing it.

"You still haven't guessed my news, so I'll tell you," he said. "We're going for an outing in the car!"

"You mean you've really got it working?" Mrs. Pepperpot could hardly believe it. "Where are we going?"

"There's a car rally over the other side of Blocksberg; it's for old cars, so I thought I might enter mine. I might even win a cup."

This was a sore point with Mr. Pepperpot. His wife knew he had always wanted to win a cup or a trophy. They did have one in the house, but she kept it hidden at the back of a cupboard, because it was one *she* had won when she was a young girl and worked on a farm. She had got it for being so good at looking after the livestock. Now she would really like Mr. Pepperpot to have one too, so she said:

"Yes, let's go. An outing would be fun, and we can take a picnic."

"I'll just go and check the engine once more; be ready in half an hour."

Mrs. Pepperpot bustled about; she was quite looking forward to seeing some new places after the long winter at home. She got out the picnic basket, hard-boiled some eggs, packed bread and butter and a piece of cold ham and some pancakes left over from last night. As she worked she made up a little song to sing in the car. This is how it went:

My hubby is mad about motoring,
Motoring, motoring,
He spends his evenings tinkering
On his rickety automobile.

So now we'll be bouncing up and down,
Up and down, up and down,
Everything is thrown in the back seat
Of the rickety automobile!

I may be crazy to go with him,
Go with him, go with him,
But oh, he's made it look so trim,
His rickety automobile!

At least we'll have a fine picnic,
A fine picnic, a fine picnic,
With sausages, bread and ham and chick
In his rickety automobile!

And then of course we'll see the sights,
See the sights, see the sights,
Of valleys and forests and mountain heights
From his rickety automobile!

Hooray!

Mr. Pepperpot grumbled when she brought the loaded basket out to the car. "What do we want with all that stuff? Much better to buy ice cream as we go along and there are plenty of roadstands where we can have a hot dog and ketchup." He liked to show that he knew what tourists did when they went motoring.

"No nourishment in ice cream," said Mrs. Pepperpot. "And I don't trust roadstands." With that she dumped the basket in the back seat and got in.

Mr. Pepperpot got in the driving seat. But just before he started the engine he had a sudden thought: "You won't *shrink* while we're out, will you?"

"Oh, stop fussing!" said Mrs. Pepperpot, as she settled herself comfortably. "You know I never have any idea when it's going to happen. If it does, it does, and I usually manage, don't I? Start up, Mr. P., I'm quite looking forward to this outing!"

So off they went. At first Mr. Pepperpot drove very carefully down the little country road from the house. But once they were on the main road with its smooth asphalt surface, he put his foot on the pedal and they hummed along at quite a good pace. He started to whistle; Mr. Pepperpot always did that when he was happy.

"This is the life!" he sang. "All these years I've been mucking about with an old horse and cart, never getting anywhere, never seeing anything."

"I don't know," said Mrs. Pepperpot, "you used to get around quite well on a bicycle—fast enough to break your neck!"

"Yes, but think of the advantages of a motorcar:

four wheels, comfortable seats, plenty of room for luggage and a roof to keep the rain out."

"Plenty of expense too," answered Mrs. Pepperpot, "and plenty of time needed for repairs. When will you ever get around to clearing the drains or help me dig up potatoes now?"

"Stop grumbling and enjoy yourself!" ordered Mr.

Pepperpot as he slowed down over a little bridge. On the other side there was a stand selling ice cream.

"There, didn't I tell you we could get ice cream?" said Mr. Pepperpot. "I'll go and get you one." So he hopped out of the car and went over to the stand to buy a double vanilla for Mrs. Pepperpot. "That should put her in a good mood," he said to himself,

as he balanced his way back toward the car with it.
But halfway there he was distracted by a hissing noise
in the grass at his feet.

"Oops!" he said, and dropped the beautiful ice
cream!

There was nothing for it but to go back for another.

He paid his money and the girl gave him a second ice cream as big as the first. Back he went, holding the cone with its great mound on top very steady. But as he passed the place where he had spilled the first one, he made the mistake of looking down. And do you know? The ice cream on the ground was *moving!* Poor Mr. Pepperpot dropped the second cone on the first one and fled back to the stand. He was sure there was a snake in the grass, and he was very much afraid of snakes.

But back at the stand a bus-load of travelers had just lined up for refreshments and Mr. Pepperpot had to stand at the end of the line.

And what was going on down there in the grass
where two double ice creams were bubbling and
churning like boiling porridge? You've guessed it—Mrs.
Pepperpot was underneath! She had got out of the
car to stretch her legs and then, suddenly, she had
shrunk to the size of a pepperpot!

There she was, right in Mr. Pepperpot's path; she
was so afraid he might step on her that she hissed
like a snake, and the next thing she knew, she was
struggling to get her head clear of a freezing cold
and sticky mess! She had only just started breathing
again when dollop! She was covered with another
portion of ice cream as big, cold and sticky as the first!

Poor Mrs. Pepperpot didn't know what to do; she'd never be able to dig her way out alone. "I'll just freeze to death," she thought miserably. But after a little while she felt the load of ice cream growing lighter, and soon she could push her head through.

"That's better!" she said.

"It's jolly good!" said a voice next to her, and there stood a young kitten, licking his chops and purring.

"What a beautiful, clever little pussy you are!" cried Mrs. Pepperpot, wiping the ice cream from her face.

"Mm, can't say *you're* exactly beautiful, but you taste very good," said the kitten. "Are you made of

ice cream right through? I mean, will I be able to eat you all up?"

"Certainly not!" cried Mrs. Pepperpot. "Ice cream right through indeed! What an idea! No, my friend, I'm just an ordinary woman most of the time. But now and then I shrink to this size. Come to think of it, I don't mind if you do lick me clean—help yourself!"

The kitten set to work very willingly. He was so thorough that soon Mrs. Pepperpot had to shout to him to stop.

"I'm very ticklish, you see," she said, laughing. "Fancy me getting a cat-lick; I never expected that when we set off in the car this morning."

"You have a car?" asked the kitten.

"My husband does; we're on an outing—or we were till this happened. Where do you live?"

The kitten hung his head. "Nowhere, really. I did live in a barn with my mother, but some people came along and picked me up. They took me back to their house and gave me lots of food—that's where I got my taste for ice cream. They used to play with me and at night they would tuck me up in a little basket. It was a wonderful life!"

"What happened then?"

"Well, they didn't belong in this place—they were just on vacation. So suddenly, yesterday, they packed up all their stuff, locked the door of the house and got in their car and drove off. I thought I was going too, of course, but they must have forgotten all about me, because they didn't even bother to look back or wave goodbye."

"I see," said Mrs. Pepperpot, looking thoughtful. "So now you have no home?"

"No," said the kitten, "there's no one to feed me or play with me or call me in at night. Until I found you and the ice cream I hadn't had anything to eat since yesterday." He licked the last bit of ice cream out of Mrs. Pepperpot's ear with the point of his rough tongue.

"It was just as well I did shrink today," said Mrs. Pepperpot. "People like that shouldn't be allowed to keep pets. Animals are not just playthings for children to throw away when they don't need them any more. Fancy going off and not even asking a neighbor to look after you!" Mrs. Pepperpot was getting really worked up, as she always did when people were thoughtless or unkind to animals.

The kitten was watching her with his head on one side. "Couldn't you take me home with you and let me be your pussy? You're fond of animals, aren't you? And you can talk cat language."

"Well," said Mrs. Pepperpot, "there are one or two snags. My husband is *not* very fond of animals, especially young kittens. And as to understanding cat language, I can only do that when I am small!"

"Will you grow large again soon?"

"I don't know."

"Will I be afraid of you when you do?"

Mrs. Pepperpot laughed. "I shouldn't think so. But if you could manage to carry me on your back over to that old car there, I might grow to my normal size quite soon."

"I'll try. Climb up!"

But though Mrs. Pepperpot got on his back all right, she was too heavy for the kitten to carry.

"Perhaps I could pull you along by your skirt," he suggested.

"I don't mind what you do," said Mrs. Pepperpot, as she lay down on the ground with her arms tucked under her head. "Pull away!"

The kitten took Mrs. Pepperpot's skirt between his teeth and dragged her as carefully as he could down

the path, trying to avoid the ice-cream puddle and empty cartons and drinking straws that people had dropped.

"I hope I'm not bumping you too much," said the kitten.

"Not at all," answered Mrs. Pepperpot, "I have a fine view of the sky overhead and the birds and the trees."

But now we had better see what was happening to Mr. Pepperpot. We left him in the line and he stood there a long, long time before he got served again. This time he bought the biggest possible cone and made straight for the car, looking neither up nor down, hoping Mrs. Pepperpot had not lost patience with him altogether.

"Supposing she has shrunk and I won't be able to find her?" he thought anxiously, but when he opened the back door of the car, there she sat, as large as life.

"Oh my! Am I glad to see you!" He sighed with relief.

"You sound as if I'd been to the moon and back," she said.

"Well, you see, if you had shrunk and disappeared, I'd never have got through all this ice cream." And he held out the cone.

"Get along with you—I told you to stop fussing," said Mrs. Pepperpot. She set the cone carefully into the corner of the basket.

"Aren't you going to eat it after all that?" Mr. Pepperpot sounded a little hurt.

"All in good time. We'd better be getting on now, if you're going to enter the rally."

"I'm not sure I'll bother with that car rally," he said. "While I was standing in the line at the stand I heard someone talking about a cross-country race, and it's not as far to drive as the car rally. Shall we go there instead?"

"It's all one to me," said Mrs. Pepperpot, "as long as we're enjoying ourselves."

Mr. Pepperpot beamed. "Yes, we are, aren't we?"

He didn't know that Mrs. Pepperpot meant herself and the kitten, which was safely hidden in the basket and enjoying a good lick at that giant ice cream.

Chapter Two

THE ROAD WAS smooth and they were driving along quite comfortably, when Mr. Pepperpot suddenly stopped the car.

"Did you hear something?" he asked his wife.

She shook her head. They drove on a bit further, but then he stopped again.

"Didn't you hear anything this time?" he asked.

No, she didn't, and he drove on again. But when he stopped for the third time Mr. Pepperpot said: "You must have heard it; it sounded just like a cat meowing."

"Probably your brakes have got wet," suggested Mrs. Pepperpot.

"I'll have a look," said Mr. Pepperpot and got out.

Mrs. Pepperpot stayed where she was and stroked the kitten to keep him quiet. After a while she asked her husband if he'd found anything; she knew you shouldn't rush a man when he's looking for trouble in his car.

"Not yet!" came the answer from under the hood.

"Perhaps the engine is overheated?"

"Yes, I think I'll get some water from that farm up on the hill." He took out a green plastic bucket and started trudging up the hill. He could see there was a pump in the front yard.

The farm was quite a long way off, so Mrs. Pepperpot thought she could safely take a short stroll with the kitten. The little creature was very good, running along beside her, purring and rubbing against her skirt.

"You have a better purr than the car engine," said Mrs. Pepperpot. "Oh, look! There's a pigsty. Let's go and visit the pigs."

Basking in the sunshine lay a big sow with a whole row of little piglets stretched out beside her. From time to time they woke up, pushed and nudged and sucked and squealed, then fell asleep again.

Just as she was bending over to stroke the sow, lo and behold! Mrs. Pepperpot SHRANK for the second time that day! This was most unusual and quite unexpected. Luckily, she didn't land among the pigs, but tumbled into a patch of weeds right by the sty.

"Did you hurt yourself?" asked a squeaky little voice.

"No, I don't think so, thanks," said Mrs. Pepperpot, struggling to her feet. "I'm so used to falling—it's almost second nature to me. Hullo! I thought I was talking to a kitten; now I see you're a pig!"

It was indeed a pig, but a very, very small and thin one.

"Don't you belong in there with the others?" asked Mrs. Pepperpot.

"I do really. But the farmer put me out. He said my mother had enough to feed and I would have to fend for myself, unless . . ." The piglet put his head on one side and looked wistfully at Mrs. Pepperpot from under his white eyelashes, ". . . unless some nice person would take me home and feed me with a bottle."

"Poor little mite! Does *nobody* want you?"

"Not so far. They all come and look at my mother

and the others, gobbling away. But when they see me they just shake their heads and go away," said the little pig.

"They're stupid and unkind!" said Mrs. Pepperpot, "leaving a fine little fellow like you to starve. I wish I had a bottle of milk handy. If I were my proper size, I'd take you home with me."

Here the kitten, who had been watching, chipped in. "You see, Piggy, Mrs. Pepperpot isn't always this size—a little while ago she was enormous!"

Mrs. Pepperpot laughed. "I may seem enormous to you, Kitty, but most people call me a *little* old woman. However, what we want right now is to get ourselves over to the farmer's pump. Then, when I grow large again, I can come and get you. My hus-

band's up there too, getting water for his car. But it's too far for me to walk as I am now."

"I don't think I could carry you," said the piglet, "my legs are too wobbly and weak!"

"I'll do what I did before," said the kitten, "pull you along by your skirt."

"Champion!" said Mrs. Pepperpot. "You wait here for us, Piggy. We may be some time, but we'll be back."

They set off as before, the kitten tugging and pulling Mrs. Pepperpot, bumping over the grass and stones. It was hard work up the hill, but the kitten didn't give up till they had reached the pump, where they found the green plastic bucket, but no Mr. Pepperpot. He had gone inside to chat with the farmer about the

wonders of his old car. They got so interested that when he came out he had forgotten what he came for—to fill his bucket with water.

Mrs. Pepperpot, who had hidden inside the bucket when Mr. Pepperpot and the farmer came out of the house, wondered if she was going to be left behind. But halfway down the hill Mr. Pepperpot remembered the bucket and came rushing back again. The farmer was still standing there grinning. "You won't get far without water!" he said, as Mr. Pepperpot hitched the bucket under the pump and started pumping.

Poor Mrs. Pepperpot! It wasn't very clever of her to hide in the bucket, was it? Now she was in great danger of drowning while Mr. Pepperpot went on pumping and talking to the farmer at the same time.

"Travel broadens the mind," he was saying. "You need to get out and see for yourself what a beautiful country we live in. D'you know, when I sit behind that wheel with a long clear road in front of me, it often makes me want to sing and shout . . . Ouch!" And he gave a great shout and jumped in the air!

The farmer thought he was showing him what he did when he was driving, but Mr. Pepperpot went on jumping about, the bucket fell off the hook and all the water ran out. And Mrs. Pepperpot? Well, she had decided to climb out of the bucket and had managed to get a hold on Mr. Pepperpot's trouser leg. Then, while he was still talking, she hoisted herself up as far as his suspenders, but there her foot slipped and she

gave him a kick. She also pinched him while trying to stop herself from falling. So that was why Mr. Pepperpot shouted; he thought there was an ant inside his shirt.

By now all the rest of the family had come out of the house to look at this funny man dancing around their pump. When he saw they were laughing at him, he ran down the hill to find Mrs. Pepperpot and get her to remove the ant, or whatever it was.

But there was no sign of Mrs. Pepperpot either in the car or up and down the road.

"Oh dear, oh dear! Now she's shrunk and vanished completely. What shall I do?" After he had hunted around and called her in vain, he suddenly remembered the ant. Heavens! That might have been her! He felt himself all over, but there was no sign of any creepy-crawly now. He would have to go back to the pump. Perhaps he could ask the farmer if he

had seen his wife. But how was he going to explain that she might be as small as a doll?

When he got to the pump the whole family was still standing there, so he laughed a little nervously and said, "I came back for my bucket of water."

They watched him pump it full again. Then he said, "Oh, by the way, did you see if I dropped a small doll with a striped skirt on?"

"Doll?" said the farmer. "No, I didn't see any doll. But I'll ask my wife. Have you seen the gentleman's doll, Kristina?"

"No," said his wife, "I didn't see any doll. But I'll ask my daughter." She turned to the eldest girl. "Have you seen a little doll, Gerda?"

"No," said Gerda, "I didn't see any doll. But I'll ask my younger sister, Britta. Did you see a little doll?"

"No," said Britta, "but I'll ask my smaller sister, Ada. Did you see a little doll?"

"No," said Ada, "but I'll ask my baby sister, Maggie. Did you see a little doll?"

"No," said Maggie, "but I'll ask my big brother, Jack. Did you see a little doll?"

"No," said Jack, "but I'll ask my bad brother, Ben. Did you see a little doll?"

"No," said Ben, "but I'll ask my good brother, Jim. Did you see a little doll?"

"No," said Jim, "but I'll ask my sad brother, Frank. Did you see a little doll?"

"No," said Frank, "but I'll ask my gay brother, Pete. Did you see a little doll?"

"No," said Peter, "but I'll ask my baby brother, John. Did you see a little doll?"

"No," said Baby John, "no lil' dolly at all!"

"I'm afraid we haven't seen your doll," said the farmer. Meanwhile Mr. Pepper-pot was wringing his hands and muttering to himself, "I've lost her—this time I really have lost my own dear wife!"

"Did you say *wife?*" asked the farmer with surprise. "I thought it was a doll you had lost."

"Well, you see . . . the doll . . . er . . ." Mr. Pepperpot didn't know what to say.

"If it's your *wife* you're looking for," said the farmer, slapping Mr. Pepperpot on the back, "don't worry! We saw a little old lady in a striped skirt get into your car while you were on your way back here, didn't we, Kristina?"

"Yes," said his wife, "and my daughter saw her too, didn't you, Gerda?"

But before the whole family could go through their rigamarole again, Mr. Pepperpot was off down the hill, not forgetting the green plastic bucket of water! When he got to the car, there sat Mrs. Pepperpot, patiently waiting on the back seat, with her picnic basket on her knee and a cardboard box at her feet.

Mr. Pepperpot was so relieved, he gave her a big kiss. But he couldn't help asking her: "Did you . . . did you SHRINK?"

"I don't know why you have to keep asking me about that, Mr. P.," said Mrs. Pepperpot crossly. "Try and get that car going for a change!"

This time the car gave no trouble at all of course. The bucket of water had cooled the engine. But Mr. Pepperpot still felt it would be best to have it checked at the next garage, and Mrs. Pepperpot didn't argue, as she wanted to go into the shop right beside it. There she bought a baby's bottle and nipple and a pint of milk.

"What do you want that for?" asked her husband when she came back to the car.

"Questions! Questions! When are we going to get

to that cross-country race you're so keen to go to?"

"As a matter of fact, I don't think I *am* so keen now. The man here at the garage has just told me about a fair near here where they have one of those 'trials of strength.' You know, you hit an iron plate with a big hammer as hard as you can and a disk shoots up to ring a bell. I think I'd like to have a bash at that. You'd like to go to a fair, wouldn't you?"

"I expect so. I might try winning something myself," said Mrs. Pepperpot.

So off they went again: Mr. Pepperpot, Mrs. Pepperpot, one kitten and one piglet, which, up to now, had kept very quiet.

Chapter Three

THEY DROVE ON for a while. Mr. Pepperpot kept looking out for posters to show where the fair was being held. In the back seat Mrs. Pepperpot had made up a little song to keep them amused. This is how it went:

> *I know a little pussy-kitten,*
> *With shiny coat and snowy mitten,*
> *His ice-cream whiskers wrapped in a rug,*
> *He's safe inside my basket snug.*

"I like to hear you sing," said Mr. Pepperpot, "it shows you're feeling happy. I know the tune, too, but I don't remember those words."

"You're not likely to. I just made them up!" she answered. "I'll sing you another verse."

> *I know a little piggy pink,*
> *With curly tail and eyes that twink,*
> *His legs are shaky, but no one mocks,*
> *He likes to sit in my old box.*

"It's a funny song, all right, and you're a funny old woman," said Mr. Pepperpot.

"Funny yourself!" said his wife. "Now I'll sing one about you. Here goes."

> *I know a man who's not a giant,*
> *But very smart and self-reliant.*
> *In motoring he'd spend his life,*
> *He only fears to lose his wife!*

"There!" shouted Mr. Pepperpot, slowing down.

"Where? What?" Mrs. Pepperpot didn't know what he was talking about.

"There's the fair. Now I can swing the Big Hammer—you'll see. I'll knock that thingummy right to the top—Ping! Let's see." He got out and read the poster. "There are lots of other attractions too—sword-swallowers and tight-rope walkers . . ."

"I'd be careful about swallowing swords, if I were you," said Mrs. Pepperpot, getting out of the car and closing the door to keep her pets in. "You make enough fuss if you get as much as a herring bone in your throat!"

"Silly! They're professionals! Well, I'm going this way to the Big Hammer. Why don't you go and look at the circus animals? They say they're as clever as people." And with that Mr. Pepperpot hurried off into the crowd.

The noise was terrific; hurdy-gurdy music from the merry-go-rounds, people screaming on the Big Wheel, bumper cars clanging and the stall-holders all trying to shout each other down.

Mrs. Pepperpot felt quite lost, and wondered where she should go. She decided to buy another ice cream for the kitten and a carton of milk for that hungry piglet. He had been sleeping quietly in his box since she gave him the first bottle, but soon he'd be awake again, and then he might squeal.

Just as she reached the stand, Mrs. Pepperpot felt the ominous signs. "Not again!" was all she had time to say before she shrank and found herself rolling on the ground with huge boots and shoes tramping all around her.

Was she scared! There was danger from every direction, and she was at her wits' end. Should she try and climb up someone's trouser leg? Before she could make a grab, however, she found herself picked up by her skirt and whisked away from the tramping feet. Whatever it was, it ran so fast that poor Mrs. Pepperpot was slung from side to side and completely lost her breath. She tried to shout "Let me go!" but then she realized it would be better to let herself get carried out of harm's way. Finally, behind a big tent, whatever-it-was stopped and she felt herself lowered

carefully onto the grass. Looking up, she saw standing over her a furry creature with black, floppy ears and a big mustache.

"Hullo," she said. "What are you supposed to be?"

"Oh," said the creature, "I'm just me!"

Mrs. Pepperpot laughed. "I see! I ought to have known. Of course, you're a puppy. Perhaps you're one of those clever circus dogs trained to do tricks?"

"No one's going to train me to do tricks!" declared the puppy, shaking his floppy ears vigorously. "I do what I want and that's that!"

"Quite right," said Mrs. Pepperpot, "I do what *I* want, too, except when I turn small like I am now. Then I have to rely on other people's help. If you can help me now, perhaps *I* can help *you* when I grow large. But I can only understand animal language when I am small, so if you've anything to tell me, you'd better do it now."

Then the puppy told her his story in little excited

barks: he really belonged to the circus manager, but when he wouldn't learn to count and to bark in the key of F major, the manager chased him out of his tent.

"But you haven't heard the worst," added the puppy.

"Let's have it," said Mrs. Pepperpot.

The puppy put his head on one side and looked at her sadly. "Are you a pedigreed?" he asked.

"Well," laughed Mrs. Pepperpot, "I've never really thought about it. I don't think I care if I am or not."

"As a dog, if you're not a pedigreed, you're useless, that's what they told me," said the puppy.

"Never mind! You have a beautiful mustache."

"They said it didn't belong with my kind of breed."

"Oh, forget about them!" said Mrs. Pepperpot. "That mustache will come in very handy, for you and I are going to fool the whole lot of them!"

The puppy looked at her with big round eyes. "Why, what are we going to do?"

"You must pick me up very carefully in your mouth, just like you did before," said Mrs. Pepperpot.

The puppy did as he was told, and picked her up most gently. Mrs. Pepperpot draped his long mustache over her skirts and legs, so that she was completely hidden. "Now jump straight onto the roof of that caravan!" she said.

It was a most tremendous leap, but the puppy arrived safely with Mrs. Pepperpot in his mouth. At first no one noticed them up there, but when the music stopped for a pause Mrs. Pepperpot suddenly started to sing through the puppy's mustache:

Baa, baa, black sheep,
Here we go gathering nuts in May,
Who killed Cock Robin?
Three blind mice, three blind mice,

Little Tommy Tucker,
Sing a song of sixpence,
Girls and boys come out to play,
See saw, Marjorie Daw.

Wasn't that an old jumble of a song? But it was the best she could do, hanging there in mid-air. The people standing around the caravan were astonished

to see a puppy on the roof, and even more amazed
that he was singing. Others joined them to watch. The
merry-go-round came to a halt, the passengers left the
bumper cars, and even the circus performance stopped
as the audience flocked outside to hear the clever
puppy sing.

The circus manager himself appeared. "Hi!" he
shouted, "that's my puppy! Here boy, here boy!" But

the puppy took no notice; it was all he could do to keep his balance with Mrs. Pepperpot in his mouth.

"Can you count to ten?" shouted the circus manager. "One?" No answer. "Two?" Silence. "Three? Four? Five?" Still no answer from the puppy. "You're just putting us on, you obstinate little brute! Six, seven, eight, nine, ten . . ."

Mrs. Pepperpot decided it was time to teach that circus manager a lesson. In a high, yappy voice she said quickly, "Eleven, twelve, thirteen, fourteen, fifteen, sixteen, seventeen, eighteen, nineteen, twenty!"

Consternation in the crowd! The circus manager jumped up and down, whooping with excitement. There was such a crush of people trying to see the puppy, that they overturned the caravan and everyone fell on top of everyone else! When at last they had

sorted themselves out, the puppy had disappeared. He and Mrs. Pepperpot had jumped clear when the caravan toppled, and had made for the car as fast as his little legs could carry them.

When Mr. Pepperpot returned, his wife, who was now her proper size, was wrapping something up in an old coat they kept in the back of the car.

Mr. Pepperpot was so excited about the singing puppy, he didn't notice what she was doing. "You should have heard him—he sang a whole song!"

Mrs. Pepperpot laughed. "Get along with you! A dog singing!"

"I saw him with my own eyes!" he assured her. Then he looked thoughtful for a moment and said, "Come to think of it, it was rather like one of your songs!"

"Was it, indeed?" Mrs. Pepperpot looked pained. "How did you get on with the Big Hammer?"

"With all that fuss about the puppy, I didn't get time to try it. Anyway, I heard someone talking about a walking contest. So I thought I'd drive a little farther and try that."

"Very well," said Mrs. Pepperpot with a sigh. She was beginning to wonder if they'd ever get home that day. If they had to stay overnight somewhere, what would she do with the animals?

But Mr. Pepperpot drove happily on, and in the back seat—though he didn't know it—he now had *four* passengers: Mrs. Pepperpot, the kitten, the piglet and the puppy with black floppy ears and a big mustache.

Chapter Four

WHEN THEY HAD DRIVEN another few miles Mr. Pepperpot stopped the car.

"I don't know what's wrong," he said, "but the car seems so heavy at the back. Perhaps the tires are going flat. I think I'd better pump them up a bit. You'll have to get out meanwhile."

Mrs. Pepperpot didn't like this idea. If her husband started rummaging in the back of the car he might find the animals.

"I don't feel like getting out just now," she said. "Can't it wait till you get to the next gas station? Then they can do it for you."

"I suppose so," he said and drove on. But soon he was grumbling again: "Why can't you sit still? If there's not enough room for you in the back seat, you could throw out some of that food."

He didn't know that the food had been eaten up long ago by the piglet, the kitten and the puppy.

"If anything's to be thrown out, it's not the food!" said Mrs. Pepperpot quite huffily. "If your old car can't even carry one passenger, Mr. P., *I* can get out, and you can go on alone!"

This was very cunning of Mrs. Pepperpot, because if there is one thing a proud car owner hates, it is criticism of his beautiful automobile.

"You stay right where you are!" said Mr. Pepperpot. "It's not really the weight that matters, but all the strange noises I have been hearing from the back. I must find out what's causing them."

"Oh dear!" sighed Mrs. Pepperpot, "that must have been my singing you could hear. I was making

up a sort of song—not a proper one, you understand, for *I* have never sung in a choir like *you* . . ."

Mr. Pepperpot brightened up at the word "choir," as he had been very good at choir-singing when he was young.

"That's right, my dear," he said, "not everyone is born with a beautiful voice. But you go right ahead and sing. Nothing like it for uplifting the soul and making us think of the joys of spring!"

"Don't know so much about the joys of spring," muttered Mrs. Pepperpot, "it's more like a farmyard when I get going. But you asked for it."

> *Dogs are lots of fun,*
> *When they jump and run,*
> *But when they start to yap-yap,*
> *They will get a slap-slap!*
>
> *Cats are sweet and furry,*
> *Never in a hurry,*
> *Till they start a row-row,*
> *Fight and scratch and meow-meow!*
>
> *As for little pigs,*
> *See them dancing jigs;*
> *Their little feet go boink-boink,*
> *While their snouts go oink-oink!*

"Ridiculous!" was Mr. Pepperpot's comment. "This time I didn't even know the tune."

"Nor did I when I started," said Mrs. Pepperpot. "I can see a gas station over there."

"Good," said Mr. Pepperpot. He stopped at the

garage and asked the man to pump up his tires, and
Mrs. Pepperpot hoped the animals would keep quiet
meanwhile. But she needn't have worried, for her
husband was soon deep in conversation with the
garage man about a fishing competition which was
due to start at two o'clock.

"You can put your name on the list," the man was
saying, "and then I'll show you which way to go."

Mr. Pepperpot signed his name to show he was
a competitor, and they set off again, this time down a
narrow lane through a wood. It was lovely and cool in
there and soon they got to a little green glade.

"This is where the man said I could park the car,"
said Mr. Pepperpot. He got out and fetched his

fishing tackle from the trunk. "I suppose you don't want to come and watch me?"

"I'd rather wait for you to bring me back a lovely fish for my supper. I'll just lie in the nice grass and watch the trees for a bit."

"Bye, bye, then," said Mr. Pepperpot, walking off toward the river, hopeful as ever.

Mrs. Pepperpot called "Good luck!" after him, but as soon as he was out of sight she opened the basket to let the kitten out, lifted the piglet from the carton and unrolled the puppy, who had been having a nice nap inside the old coat. They all came tumbling out on the grass. At first the kitten was a bit frightened and arched his back and hissed at the puppy, but soon they were all three chasing each other round and round. Mrs. Pepperpot sat on a tree stump in the middle and enjoyed the fun. When she thought they had had enough exercise she caught them all and put them back in the car.

"Be good," she told them. "I'm going to the shop on the main road to buy some more food for you." And she shut the car door securely.

It was very pleasant walking along the quiet lane, and she was quite sorry to get back onto the dusty road. Luckily, the shop wasn't far. It was one of those old-fashioned country stores where they sell everything from pickled herrings in barrels to hair nets, barbed wire and licorice. There were a lot of people waiting to be served, so she took a stroll around the back, where she found a chicken yard. She counted twelve fine hens, pecking and scraping in the sand, but over in a corner stood a miserable little bird, blinking her eyes and shivering. She looked so bedraggled and thin, that Mrs. Pepperpot at once felt sorry for her.

"You poor thing! But don't you worry, I'll have

you out of here in no time, as sure as my name's Pepperpot!"

The little hen didn't seem to hear her, but Mrs. Pepperpot went back inside and bought her provisions. When she had finished she asked the little man behind the counter if he would sell her the hen.

"Oh, you don't want that miserable creature!" he exclaimed. "She's never been any good at laying eggs, and now she's getting old and tough, too."

"We none of us get any younger," said Mrs. Pepperpot, "and she hasn't had much of a chance, being chased around the yard from morning till night." As you know, when Mrs. Pepperpot makes up her mind she can be very determined, and at last the little man gave in. He found a big cardboard box and put the hen in it. She was so scared she lay absolutely still.

Mrs. Pepperpot left the shop with the cardboard box under one arm and the basket of food under the other. It was quite a heavy load for her to carry, and when she reached the lane she put both down, so that she could change hands and have a rest. Also she

wanted to see if the hen was all right. She lifted the lid just a little.

"Mercy!" she shouted, for at that moment she SHRANK for the *fourth* time that day and toppled in with the hen!

More frightened than ever, the bird struggled out of the box, but Mrs. Pepperpot managed to cling onto one of her legs. This stopped the hen from flying away.

"Whoa!" said Mrs. Pepperpot. "Stand still while

I get on your back." The hen was squawking, and as soon as Mrs. Pepperpot was on her back she ran as fast as she could into the bushes, where she got stuck.

"You're a scatter-brain and no mistake!" Mrs. Pepperpot told her when they were out in the lane again.

"That's what they've all said—ever since I was born," said the hen sadly.

Mrs. Pepperpot patted her neck. "I'm sorry, I didn't mean to hurt your feelings. Don't you bother what people say. From now on you're coming to live with me and be my very special feathered friend."

"Thanks very much, but would you tell me where we are going and how we are going to get anywhere with you such a very small person?"

"All right. I want you to take me along this lane till we get to my husband's car. I'm not this size all the time, you see, and should be back to normal human shape soon."

"Well, I hope you hurry up, because I can see the fox over there in the bushes!" said the hen, blinking her eyes nervously in that direction. Sure enough! There stood Master Fox, and he was licking his chops.

"Don't worry," whispered Mrs. Pepperpot, "I'll deal with him!" Out loud she said, "I see a certain well-known person is out for a walk in the sunshine."

"That's right. I was giving myself an appetite for my dinner. But I seem to be in luck," laughed the fox, "as my dinner is out walking too!" And he made ready to spring on the hen.

"Hold on!" shouted Mrs. Pepperpot. "Don't be in too much of a hurry, Master Fox. You see, I'm going around with invitations to a picnic, so I may as well invite you too. That is, if you'll behave like a gentleman."

"Very funny!" said the fox, showing his teeth. "Of course you thought you could trick me like the rooster once did when he got me to wash my paws before I started eating. I know that one!" He put one paw on the hen, who was trembling all over by now.

But Mrs. Pepperpot kept calm. "I'm not trying to trick you," she said. "If you'll let go of the hen at once, I promise you'll have a meal much better than a tough old bird. But first I want you to carry the basket of groceries over to that car in the glade. Then you can come back and fetch me and the hen."

"Oh no!" cackled the hen, more terrified than ever.

"Another trick!" said the fox. "When I get back you'll both be gone. I want my food *now!*" He put the other paw on Mrs. Pepperpot's skirt.

"How stupid you are!" said Mrs. Pepperpot. "I've always heard that foxes were so smart, but that must have been in the old days. If you're afraid of losing us, the hen can carry me on her back and we'll walk beside you all the way."

The fox agreed. He took the basket in his mouth and the hen carried Mrs. Pepperpot on her back till they reached the car. Once there, Mrs. Pepperpot

asked the fox to unpack the food and sent the hen up on the roof of the car to fetch a plastic tablecloth which they spread on the grass.

"When do we start the feast?" asked the fox.

"We'll have to wait till I collect the rest of the guests," said Mrs. Pepperpot. Then she put her hand to her mouth and shouted with all her might, "Are you there, Great Cat Tiger Claws?"

"Meow!" said a little voice from the car.

"What's this?" demanded the fox. "Are there other guests invited?"

"Oh yes!" answered Mrs. Pepperpot, putting her

hand to her mouth again. "Are you there, Wild Boar Gory Fangs?" she shouted as loudly as she could.

"Oink! Oink!" came the reply from the car.

"Good heavens! Are there any more?" The fox was beginning to look nervous.

"Wait and see!" said Mrs. Pepperpot. "Are you there Handlebar Mustachio Foxhunter?"

"Woof! Woof!" answered the puppy.

"Thanks very much!" said the fox, "I don't think I fancy this picnic after all!"

"Oh, come on! They'll all be very pleased to see you," said Mrs. Pepperpot. "You just sit down and enjoy yourself. The hen can sit next to you if you like."

"I'd rather not!" said the poor hen, who didn't trust the fox one inch.

The fox looked hurt. "You've tricked me just like the others," he said. But Mrs. Pepperpot shook her head.

"No. I promised you food, and I keep my promises. You can put a large chunk of ham and some fresh eggs in the basket and take it away to eat. Will that satisfy you?"

"Very generous, I'm sure," said the fox, collecting the food in the basket and picking it up. Just as he was about to run off with it, Mrs. Pepperpot said, "Just a minute! One thing more. I want the basket back."

"All right," said the fox, "if you can keep your promises, I can keep mine. I'll see you get it back." With that he vanished in the bushes, much to the hen's relief.

At that moment Mrs. Pepperpot grew to her proper size. She lost no time in getting her pets out and they all had a lovely picnic in the grass. She had just finished putting them back in their different hiding places when Mr. Pepperpot returned from his fishing contest. But she could see from his face that there would be no fish for supper *that* night.

"What happened?" she asked.

"Oh," he said despondently, "it wasn't much of a turnout. We had an hour for the contest, but I never

got a single bite. And then something very strange happened."

"What was that?"

"Well, you see this basket?" He held up a basket still dripping with water. "D'you recognize it?"

"It's our picnic basket," she said.

"That's right! What I want to know is: how did it come to be floating down-stream toward me when you are here, much farther down the river?" Mr. Pepperpot was scratching his head and looking very puzzled.

Mrs. Pepperpot could hardly stop herself from laughing, but she just said, "I have no idea! How did you get it back?"

"It floated straight onto my line, so I hooked it out."

"Life's full of surprises, isn't it?" said Mrs. Pepperpot, getting back in the car. "Now let's get on, Mr.
P., or we'll never get home today."

So Mr. Pepperpot turned the car out of the little
glade and drove off with Mrs. Pepperpot, the kitten,
the piglet, the puppy and the hen all on the back seat.

Chapter Five ,

THEY HAD NOT GONE many miles when Mr. Pepperpot put his foot on the brake and stopped very sharply.

"*Now* what's up?" asked Mrs. Pepperpot, who had been having a little nap.

"There's a poster about a contest," said Mr. Pepperpot. "I want to see what it says."

"Don't you think we've had enough contests for today? We're getting tired and it's time to go home."

"Speak for yourself, Mrs. P. I'm not tired," said Mr. Pepperpot.

"Anyway, I wish you wouldn't put the brakes on so suddenly, you should think of us in the back seat," said Mrs. Pepperpot.

"Us? Who's us?" he asked.

"Why . . . er . . . the baggage and me!" Mrs. Pepperpot was a little flustered—she had nearly given the game away! But her husband had now got out of the car to look at the poster, and this is what it said:

SENSATIONAL SPORTS EVENT TODAY

The Great Traditional
Cross-Country Race
Starting from Railway Square
at 4 p.m.
The Course is as Follows:

Cross Bilberry Marsh by
mapped-out Route,
Wade over Black River
above the Waterfall,
Take 12 ft leap from Red Cliff
on the North Bank to
White Rock on the South Bank,
Run to finishing line at
the Big Spruce Tree.

1st PRIZE A SILVER CUP
Refreshments Served

"Mercy me!" said Mrs. Pepperpot when her husband read it out. "You're not thinking of entering that one, are you?"

"Well, I don't know," he said, "I'd like to watch it anyway."

"And what are we going to do meanwhile?" she asked.

Mr. Pepperpot stared at her. "You said 'we' again!"

"Oh well!" she said crossly. "You keep stopping and starting, and messing about. Is it any wonder if I get mixed up? What am I going to do, then? Sit in this stuffy old car?"

"No. As you say you're tired, I'll drop you at the station and you can take the train home."

Mrs. Pepperpot thought this over, but then she agreed. "As long as you leave the car in the station yard and promise me not to take part in the stupid competition," she said.

He promised and drove the car to the station where he parked it. He gave Mrs. Pepperpot some money to get home and then he went around the other side to the Railway Square to watch the competitors line up for the race.

When he was out of sight Mrs. Pepperpot went over to the ticket office. There she bought a ticket for herself and paid for the animals to be put in a wooden crate, so that they could travel in the baggage car. A nice conductor helped her get the animals in.

"I'll stay with them till the train comes," she told the conductor, and sat down on the crate. But just as

the train pulled up at the platform poor Mrs. Pepperpot did her fifth SHRINKING for that day! The crate had wide gaps between the boards, and Mrs. Pepperpot fell straight through onto the kitten's tail!

"Meow!" said the kitten, "that hurt!"

"Sssh! Don't make a noise," said Mrs. Pepperpot, "just try and hide me—I don't want the conductor to see me like this!"

The animals did their best. The kitten curled his tail over her dress, the puppy spread one ear over her blouse and the hen held one wing carefully over her face. The pig just stretched out beside her and blinked at her from under his white eyelashes. When the conductor came back he lifted the crate into the baggage car. Then he looked around for the old woman; where could she have gone? It was only a little train, so he looked into all the carriages and asked the stationmaster if he had seen her. She was nowhere.

But the train couldn't wait, so the conductor blew his whistle and off they went. The animals were delighted to have Mrs. Pepperpot with them. "How lucky you shrank just now!" they said.

"Well, you'd better make the most of me while you have me," she told them. "After five shrinkings in one day I don't suppose it will happen again for a long time. So, if you have any questions, fire away!"

The animals all lined up like a row of school children with Mrs. Pepperpot as their very small teacher standing out in front.

The kitten began. "Please, ma'am, when do we get to your house?"

"In time for supper," said Mrs. Pepperpot firmly,

but to herself she added "I hope," for she wondered what would happen when they got to their station.

"What am I going to have to eat?" asked the piglet.

"Don't worry, there's a whole bin of lovely mash for piglets at my house," she assured him.

"What about dogs?" asked the puppy. "Can I do as I like?"

"Certainly!" said Mrs. Pepperpot. "Liberty Hall, that's what they call my place!"

The hen looked anxiously at her. "Will there be a lot of other hens in your yard? Will they peck me?"

"You shall be my one and only special hen, didn't I tell you?" said Mrs. Pepperpot.

All the animals clapped and flapped and stamped and shouted, "Hooray for Mrs. Pepperpot!"

To keep them from getting too boisterous and to while away the time she decided to teach them a song. "Listen carefully," she said, "and join in when I point to you." She began to sing:

> *Children all, now gather round,*
> *And let us make a jolly sound,*
> *First a dog and then a cat,*
> *A little pig, a hen, all pat!*
>
> *Here we go: sing as I do,*
> *Puppy dog, a bark from you!*
> *Woof, woof! Woof, woof!*

Here she pointed to the puppy and he barked as loudly as he could, "Woof, woof! Woof, woof!"

Here we go: sing as I do,
Little Puss, a song from you!
Meow, meow! Meow, meow!

The kitten didn't wait to be asked, but sang in chorus with Mrs. Pepperpot, "Meow, meow! Meow, meow!"

Here we go: sing as I do,
Piglet, we must hear from you!
Oink, oink! Oink, oink!

When Mrs. Pepperpot pointed at him, the piglet got so carried away, he wouldn't stop "oinking," and the puppy had to give him a sharp nip.

Here we go: sing as I do,
Hennypen, a cluck from you!
Cluck, cluck! Cluck, cluck!

But the hen was so frightened by all the noise the others had made, she only managed a very small "cluck, cluck!" the first time. However, they went on practicing, and by the time the train stopped at their station, they were all singing very well indeed.

The conductor opened the door and lifted the crate onto a platform with a lot of milk cans. As nobody else got out of the train he blew the whistle and it moved off. Luckily Mrs. Pepperpot's name and address were written on the lid, so, when Peter, the milkman, came in his van to fetch the cans, he saw the crate and thought he was supposed to deliver it together

with the milk. This saved Mrs. Pepperpot a lot of
trouble, for as soon as he had put the crate down at the
corner of the road leading to her house and had
driven off, there was an almighty CRASH!

As you see in the picture, Mrs. Pepperpot grew so
fast that she burst right through the crate, scattering
the animals and the boards pell-mell all around. Such
a to-do! The hen landed on the branch of a tree, the
puppy rolled down the hill, the piglet got his snout
stuck in a hole and the poor kitten fell in the stream!

When Mrs. Pepperpot had picked herself up she
quickly collected all the animals. She put the hen
under one arm and the piglet under the other and

called the kitten and the puppy to follow her. All together they climbed the hill to her house.

"Here we are, children, home at last!" she said, as she opened the door, and set the hen and the piglet down. The kitten and the puppy trotted in after her and now they were all nosing around to see what their new home was like.

Mrs. Pepperpot sat down. She had a problem. Mr. Pepperpot was bound to come home soon. How was she going to tell him about the additions to their family? She put her finger on her nose and thought. Then she cried, "I've got it! I have a solution!"

First she put the kitten in the bed and covered him with the blanket. Then she put the piglet in the empty woodbox by the stove and sprinkled wood-shavings all over him. The puppy she hid in a basket under the table, and the hen she lifted up on the bureau. "You keep very still," she told her. "I'm going to cover you up." And she put a large lampshade over her. Then she put the coffee on and went outside to see if her husband was coming.

There he was, struggling up the hill, looking so downcast that she had to shout and wave to him to let him know she was there. When he did see her his whole face lit up and he fairly sprinted up the last bit of the road.

"Am I glad you're here!" he said, giving her a big kiss.

"Why shouldn't I be here, Mr. P.?" said Mrs. Pepperpot. "What have you done with the car?"

"I couldn't very well take it through the bog and jump it over the river, could I?"

Mrs. Pepperpot threw up her hands in horror. "You never went in for that race did you? After promising. . . ?"

"I know. I only meant to watch it. But then I heard the train conductor asking people if they'd seen a little old woman who was supposed to be traveling on the train to our station. He said she'd disappeared. So, of course, I thought at once it must be you who had turned small."

"What happened then?" she asked.

"Well, I tried to jump on the train, which was just pulling out, but I couldn't catch it. So I headed straight for Bilberry Marsh. I knew it was a short-cut and it would have taken much longer to drive the car around by the road."

"Go on!" said Mrs. Pepperpot, all ears.

"The path across the marsh was clearly marked for the race and it took me straight to the place above the waterfall where you have to wade across. Then I scrambled down the other side till I got to Red Cliff."

Mrs. Pepperpot's eyes were popping out of her head by now. "You didn't take the twelve-foot leap to White Rock, did you?"

"Of course I did. There was no other way!"

"Then you must have won the race!" said Mrs. Pepperpot. "Did they give you the Prize Cup?"

"I didn't wait for anything like that. All I was think-ing about was getting to the station in time to get you out of the train. But I was too late and I thought I'd never see you again."

"Silly!" said Mrs. Pepperpot, but she was wiping her eyes with her apron and sniffing a little. "Come on in and have some coffee."

When he was sitting comfortably with his cup of coffee she patted his cheek and said, "Thanks for the outing. I enjoyed it!"

He smiled. "I'm glad! And you didn't shrink, did you?"

"Well . . . er . . . actually I did—five times in all."

"You SHRANK FIVE TIMES???" Mr. Pepperpot looked thunderstruck.

Mrs. Pepperpot decided to tell him the whole story. "The first time I was very frightened in case you should leave me behind."

"You know I'd never do that!" said Mr. Pepperpot.

She smiled at him. "No, you wouldn't, would you? Not many people have such kind husbands as I have. Well, the first time I shrank I met a kitten. The family he belonged to had gone back to town and left him—just like that—with no food or shelter. Would you have done that?"

"No indeed, that's a terrible thing to do!" said Mr. Pepperpot.

"I knew that's how you would feel. So I thought it best to take the kitten along with me. Pussy! Pussy! You can come out now and meet your new master!"

"Meow!" said the kitten and stuck his little head out from the blanket.

"Well, I'll be . . . !" said Mr. Pepperpot. But Mrs. Pepperpot was already hurrying him back into the kitchen. "The second time I shrank," she said, "I met a piglet. That was when you went to get water from the pump, remember?"

"So it *was* you and not an ant climbing up my trouser leg?"

"It was. But never mind that. The little pig had been thrown out by the farmer to fend for himself, and he was so miserable I *had* to help him. I mean, *I've* never had to go hungry in my life—have you?"

"Well, no, I suppose I haven't . . ." said Mr. Pepperpot, scratching his head.

"There you see, I knew you would agree. Come on, Piggy, show your curly tail to Mr. Pepperpot!" And out of the shavings in the woodbox came first a pair

of pink ears, then a little pink snout, and lastly a whole pink piglet.

"Good gracious!" said Mr. Pepperpot.

"But that's not all," said his wife. "The third time I shrank was at the fair. There I was, right on the ground under all those people's feet . . ."

Mr. Pepperpot was holding his ears. "Stop! Don't tell me! One of these days you'll get yourself killed."

"Ah, but I was rescued by a very clever puppy, one that had you all gasping with his singing and his counting."

"No! You don't mean to say that that was you as well?"

Mrs. Pepperpot nodded. "But I think it's more important that a dog should be a real dog and not learn circus tricks—a dog that can be your friend and protect you."

"You mean we ought to have a guard dog?" said Mr. Pepperpot.

"That's right, and I have the very one. Out you come, Puppy! Show your master how clever you are!"

"Woof! Woof!" barked the puppy excitedly, as he danced around Mr. Pepperpot's feet.

"You see, he's your friend already," said Mrs. Pepperpot, as her husband bent down to pat the floppy black ears and pull that long mustache. "Good dog!" he said.

"The fourth time was when you were fishing. I had

gone to the shop for some groceries, and I bought a hen because she didn't lay eggs."

"Because she *didn't* lay eggs?" Mr. Pepperpot was getting quite confused.

"Well no, you see, she was being hen-pecked by all the other birds in the yard, so she didn't really have a chance."

"Cluck-cluck-cluck-a-ooooh!" The sound came from under the lampshade. Mrs. Pepperpot hurried to take it off, and there stood the hen on the bureau, and under her lay a large, brown egg!

Mr. Pepperpot burst out laughing. "She's certainly making up for lost time!"

"She laid it specially for you!" said Mrs. Pepperpot. "Because you're the kindest and most understanding of husbands, and all the animals love you!"

"Oh, no!" protested Mr. Pepperpot. "You know

very well it's you the animals love. You must have the first egg!"

"I don't care what you say, this one's going to be fried for you!" And she cracked it on the edge of the frying pan while Mr. Pepperpot watched. Into the hot fat fell *two* golden yolks!

"That hen knows how to keep the peace," said Mr. Pepperpot. "Now we can each have an egg!"

When they had had their supper Mrs. Pepperpot said, "I have one more surprise for you."

Mr. Pepperpot groaned. "Not another animal, I hope."

"Come into the parlor and I'll show you," she said and opened the door. There on the table stood a brightly polished silver cup.

"That's for you!" she said. "You've certainly earned it today."

"But that's the cup you won for handling livestock when you were a young girl working on the farm!"

"Well, I give it to you now because you're just as good at handling livestock!" answered Mrs. Pepperpot.

"I suppose we could hold it jointly . . . ?" suggested Mr. Pepperpot.

"That's a very good idea. And now, have you thought what you will do with the rest of your vacation?" she asked him.

"I can't say I have, but I don't think I'll do any more driving."

"Good!" said Mrs. Pepperpot. "I think it's very nice to stay at home sometimes. And then you can get out your tool box and build a pen for the piglet, a run for the hen, a kennel for the dog and . . ."

"And *nothing* for the cat!" said Mr. Pepperpot firmly. But the kitten didn't mind. He was already stretched out in his favorite spot—along the top of Mr. Pepperpot's armchair.

About the Author, Translator and Illustrator

Alf Prøysen, who is one of Scandinavia's best-known writ-ers for children, combines originality and humor with a real understanding of a child's love of make-believe. His "Mrs. Pepperpot" stories are now considered classics among stories for children.

The stories have been imaginatively translated by *Mari-anne Helweg*, who is well-known in England as a writer and broadcaster. The artist for all the "Mrs. Pepperpot" books, *Björn Berg*, is one of Sweden's best-known illus-trators, and once again, he has simply and amusingly portrayed the unique Mrs. Pepperpot.